THE QUIET
DISORDER

THE QUIET DISORDER

Stories By

Matthew Gallant

Paridime Press
Seattle

Copyright © 2013 by Matthew E. Gallant

ISBN-13: 978-0615818818
ISBN-10: 0615818811

Paridime Press

To all of you Fictionistas!

CONTENTS

THE QUIET DISORDER

Beyond cascading blooms of Bougainvillea, beyond pink and white petals clamoring to grasp hold of the deck rail leading down to the garden and hedge, to the sloping grass lawn to the glass windows of the greenhouse, the sun's reflecting light conspired to hide something. Nearby, underneath cloudless sky, a married couple lay on a picnic blanket and was daydreaming. Both were absorbed and content to let their thoughts roam, his not always hopeful, hers usually possessed with a desire to have things just so. Her predisposition to understand, to comprehend, to calculate the sum of all things, occupied much of her existence in the same way his was spent brooding and waiting for the worst to happen.

It was not long before a bird shrieked somewhere beyond a nearby pond in a grove of trees. The soulful cry awakened the woman. She raised herself up on one elbow and held her gaze to the pond. A branch snapped and a dark shadow moved inside a tree's golden brown canopy. She drew a deep breath, expecting to see an animal emerge from the dense foliage. In this corner of the country it was never uncommon to see deer or elk, even bear. She glanced at her husband. David was not a big man nor was he intimidating, even though his look was serious and humorless. With age his face had ruined the youthful eagerness she had fallen for and could not find now in all that he presented. She fought back a cry that had welled up in the back of her throat and threatened to erupt. She rose to her feet and carefully stepped backwards. For a moment a wave of dizziness swept over her and swirled the images in her mind, mixing them and leaving them to spill out in unpredictable order. Chaos reigned until she had the sense to turn and cross the grass lawn. She entered the greenhouse, leaving the door open behind her. It was her habit to grow flowers and as she leaned over a planter of blue lilies, staring at delicate stems, searching for signs of mold and disease, her face took on a mindless expression. She was unaware of the heavy drone of a bee lost in the soft folds of a flower's petals.

On his back, in deep thought, eyes closed, David was thinking of his wife now. Her life, and now his, had been eclipsed by entanglements, a myriad of change forced by the unnatural occurrence, the shifting of unknown elements. He wanted badly to help her, and so with a bit of reluctance he accompanied her to her doctor visits, to her Yoga class, Pilates, and core conditioning. They found themselves shopping for gluten-free foods at the natural food store in an upscale bohemian part of town. Yet, he constantly fretted over her condition, an illness that he could not comprehend or accept. He struggled with the uncertainty of her stability. He had learned with painful surprise that the smallest thing could trigger another episode.

David tried to remain optimistic, but he could not shake the feeling he had of imminent doom, a nagging notion that kept nibbling away at his inner ear. He fell into a state of concern, which he had no one to share with.

He lay there on the blanket imprisoned in his own thoughts until he had nothing more to contemplate, and got up only when the warm slow drops of rain began to tickle his bare arms and legs. A few dark clouds assembled overhead and he realized at once then the reason for his displeasure. Sarah was missing.

He found her wandering in her garden, trampling her grandifloras, her prize-winning yellow dahlias, and her blue lilies, although the flowers didn't matter. She seemed out of sorts, strange as if something invisible to him had attacked her and rendered her immobile. She did not reply to his calling her name. She moved about in ways that marked her indecisiveness, a trait he would seldom associate with her. David followed her, moving past the wood bench and the carved-out stump. He stepped over a small wrought-iron fence and among wildflowers and thickets of overgrown shrubs. She still did not notice him. He called her by name.

"Sarah."

She kept walking in this dizzy pattern, hopping about, squatting down, even picking up bunches of flowers and tossing them over her shoulder.

"Sarah."

She frowned and he knew she had heard. Her eyes twitched and he saw her become suspicious. She dropped to her knees behind an old, reclaimed wine barrel overflowing with Coleus. She knelt on the ground as though trying to conceal herself in a game of hide and seek. He stood and raised his arms into the air, thinking his presence would reduce her anxiety, but it only amplified his own concerns. His feelings about her clouded the logic of the moment. He longed for the time when he could simply reach out and she would have taken his hand. He reached out now and she misunderstood, pulling away involuntarily. She retreated and one final step towards her made her turn and head for the pond. She stepped onto the old wooden pier, marching like she was on a brisk evening walk, long arms swinging in pendulous arcs, her torso twisting back and forth as if she was trying to keep others away. A trail of purple, pink and blue petals marked her zigzag route to the end of the dock.

He called her name again and moved closer until she was within arm's reach. He picked up a pink flower next to his foot and reached for her hand, offering the flower as some symbolic greeting, a customary ritual between two strangers upon meeting. He pressed it into Sarah's hand and folded her fingers closed. He smiled at her, the child, and she opened her eyes. He cupped the soft smoothness of her chin in his palm. "Come back to me."

He lost his wife in a field of perennials. To think Sarah disappeared while tinkering in her garden was unsettling. Besides the pleasures of growing dahlias and blue lilies in the greenhouse, Sarah loved cultivating flowers in a way that others loved the smell of freshly baked bread or walks along a beach or a well-trodden path at dusk and to soak in the envious hues of a summer sunset. She seemed happiest planting tubers, topping, trimming and trying to grow plants with blooms of the largest diameter and depth possible. These were memories and now he could only visit her in his mind.

After the incident in the garden, David made arrangements to move Sarah into an Alzheimer's ward at the Broadmoor House in Seattle where her disease, fed by the close proximity of others so infected, spread like weeds. The disease mounted an offensive that required repeated efforts of challenged bravery to confront. Sarah's personal medical doctor – he had recommended Broadmoor - made his first visit Saturday morning. David was glad because Sarah always brightened with his visits. Dr. Barrow ruled over his wife with an enigmatic smile. It was his mannerism, the prospect of him not being unbearable, which had gained Sarah's attention and admiration over the many visits. Barrow was an eccentric. He actually preferred house calls to office visits. He had made several trips during a period in which Sarah's spirits rose and faltered. On this visit to Sarah's new home, Barrow was unusually reserved. David greeted him in the hallway outside Sarah's room. Barrow shook David's hand firmly and apologized for being late.

As was his usual custom, the doctor insisted he visit with Sarah alone. David saw behind the tiny oval lenses perched atop Barrow's nose that he was hesitant and perhaps his reticence to continue was meant to cheer David up. But then he went in to see Sarah, leaving David to pace outside in the hallway.

There were few people visiting at this early hour. David walked down the hall and turned the corner. He nearly collided with a nurse. Her face was distorted and she brushed by him as if he didn't matter. He was puzzled by the urgency of her movement. He was tempted to follow her. Now he was at the far end of the corridor and the third time he made the same turn he realized that, like the nurse, he was agitated. He was mirroring, in a minor way, one of his wife's stages, when she had wrung her hands, rearranged objects, repeated herself over and over.

The question now wasn't what is wrong with my wife, it's How will I continue to cope with it? What about me? There would be endless evenings alone, days without his wife's companionship. It frightened him to think about the future. What would he do with all that empty time, the hours and minutes by himself? He tried to frame that kind of solitary life in his mind and the picture was blank. Missing were the details of a lonely future – what would his life be like without her? – details missing in his mind just as the memories and the details that make us real were missing in his wife's mind. Bits and pieces of our past that we seldom realize become those precious memories that make us unique, that allow us to be loved and hated. Hate. It was so powerful. He had come to know hate with a certain amount of intimacy. Her illness wasn't Sarah's problem. It was his. Still, David hated her for what she had done to him. He didn't think about the hate too much, because he knew it would grow into something far more sinister than what it already was and that would not serve or justify a damn thing for either one of them. Barrow had mentioned this. Having thoughts like this were normal. He remembered the evening on the steps of his house, as he waited for Barrow to return to his car, and the doctor had turned and said, "It's a terrible thing, not just for what it does to her, but for what it does to you. You have to be thinking that, and I want you to know it's normal. You get frustrated, you get angry, and it will get worse. There will be times when it seems like it's Sarah's fault." And he, David, he, so arrogant, so denying, had said, "Never."

Now Barrow came out of Sarah's room.

"She's all right," Barrow explained, putting his coat back on. "She still has feelings and fears. I have given her a sedative. Not much really, just enough to calm her."

"I should have called you earlier," said David. "But this episode the other day scared me. She acted so inappropriately, confused, and contradictory."

"You're a good man, David," said Barrow softly. "While you may not understand or agree, you made the right decision. Anyway, we are here and you must now begin the adjustment phase of your life."

It was a simple statement. David let the words sink in. He could feel the pulse of blood throbbing at his temples. He was quickly growing into a man accustomed to ponderous and burdensome thoughts. And even as he was grateful to hear the doctor affirm them, he resented him, too. What good was a doctor who could not heal people?

"So, I just drop her off and let her go?"

"You have suffered enough, David," said Barrow. "Besides, you have put her into the hands of someone trained to deal with such matters and so you must now allow the caring process to begin for her. In that way, it can begin for you as well."

He remembered the sudden panicky situation in the garden, the moment he had heard the door open and shut, knowing that Sarah had escaped and was outside where she could have injured herself. She was still alive, but did she know it? Did she care?

Barrow brought his wrist up to his mouth and started to say something, but the expression on his face changed. "Time to take care of yourself."

"I don't feel like having a party," said David.

Barrow nodded. "David, this is a great paradox between the mind and the heart. It's disturbing to consider that your lifelong bond has been severed. This is not unlike experiencing the death of a spouse or even a parent. One day the person is here. The next day they are gone. You will grieve, and with grief all of your emotions are tilted on edge. There are no simple answers, but you have to try to cope with the immediate situation. You have to learn to deal with it."

David could understand that, as a doctor, he must see this kind of thing all the time. But David could not see what he was capable of. What he couldn't do.

What he wasn't strong enough to do.

"May I suggest a trip, warm sun, or fresh air, away from here," said Barrow. "Give yourself a real break. When you come back, Sarah will be here. She won't even know you were gone, really. She won't be counting hours, days, nothing like that."

Barrow proposed this notion as they walked back to the lobby. He was unexpectedly tall, stooped at the top of his back. His shoulders, narrow under a prominent chin, sloped forward and would prove difficult for any tailor. Gray hair receded and flowed over to one side in a graceful arch, exposing deep lines etched in his face, on the brow and at the corners of his eyes. David knew the doctor was trying to say something positive. He left, dashing through the rain to his car. As the white compact turned and headed out the driveway, David saw the doctor's face illuminated by one of the outside lights, an apparition leaving him stranded.

David knocked softly on her door before entering. He saw her lying on her side, facing the window. She did not move or say anything when he sat down next to her. He took her arm, which was limp and she offered no resistance. Had she lost weight? She looked thin, almost childlike, a diminutive form on the verge of disappearing completely. This terrible disease had locked her into a very small space only she occupied. He smiled at her and then commented on the nightgown she was wearing. She had picked it out at a small shop near Trafalgar Square in London, her favorite city, the year they had traveled to

England with their daughter to visit Oxford. Karen would be attending school as part of a summer internship from her local college. Sarah had been so excited to see the campus. It had been a trip full of happy memories.

Sarah turned slowly, bringing her hand to her forehead, scratching at something unseen or wanting to pull out some memory. It was the first moment for some time that they had looked each other in the eye. He almost cried out. He wanted to escape with her, leave all this sadness behind. He wanted to capture that love and keep it forever. He wanted to enjoy her laugh and see her smile. He wanted so much for them to oblige each other's whimsical desires. It's what made them a great pair.

"Hello doctor," she said.

"Listen," he said. "You're home now." He reached over to the nightstand and picked up a small photograph he had brought from home. It was a picture of Karen, with her husband, Tim, and Chase, a funny, precocious six-year-old without any inhibitions. "Here," he said. "Karen, with Tim and Chase. Last summer at the cabin."

"I can't get dressed now, sorry," she said.

"No worries," he said. "There will be plenty of time tomorrow to get dressed. You need to rest, get some sleep."

"I am tired."

"I'll go now," he said softly. "But I'll be back in the morning."

She gave him a laugh. "What on earth are you getting at? Go somewhere? I just got here."

Then he saw that she was tiring from the effects of

the sedative. He tucked the blanket gently around her shoulders. He knew she liked to be kept warm. He sat there for several minutes before he realized he was just sitting. There was nothing important in the way that he sat, but it gave him a small sense of purpose. If anything, it gave him hope.

In the morning, his wife surprised him by sitting up in bed. David introduced himself to her nurse, the same one he had seen in the hallway yesterday. Her name was Toshi. She went through the motions of checking Sarah's blood pressure, pulse, and other vital signs. David thought his wife looked tired. Toshi said she had slept all night. David asked if they would continue to give Sarah a sedative. He was concerned that lack of sleep would contribute to further bouts of depression and anxiety. Toshi would not comment on Sarah's medication, but offered her own personal view that caring for her patients meant treating them like normal adults, insisting that Sarah be allowed to make decisions and choices for herself wherever it was possible. They had ways to manage.

Toshi went over to the closet and opened it. "You have some lovely dresses, Sarah," she said.

Toshi pulled a red one from the closet and laid it out on the bed in front of Sarah.

"That's nice," said David.

Toshi smiled. She leaned in close to Sarah, trying to make contact.

"Your husband says you like this one," she said. "Would you like to get dressed now?"

David went over and pulled three other dresses from the closet. He placed these in front of Sarah and went back and pulled a pair of slacks and a sweater as well. Sarah's eyes brightened when David touched the sweater. He selected a simple pair of beige slacks and the velour sweater. Sarah stood up and removed her nightgown and underwear. She wasn't at all embarrassed to shed all her clothing. She put on the clothes and walked around the room until she caught sight of herself in front of the mirror on top of the chest. She seemed surprised to see herself. She made a frown and then a smile. She winked and then stuck out her tongue.

"There," she said, peering at her reflection as if she were near-sighted.

David observed his wife: one real Sarah and the other fake, neither depicting the Sarah he remembered. She looked tired, as if her body couldn't hold her up anymore. As long as she lay down, she looked okay. Her hands were clasped together in front and she was not wearing any jewelry. She spotted him looking and shoved her hands in her pockets. She gave a sort of half-nod, accepting herself for the time being. He wondered what she really saw when she looked at herself.

She went over to the window and pulled back the curtain. "After I get dressed," she said. "I'll want to go to the store for our trip."

"Fine," said David. For a moment, he wanted to get her things and take her home. He wanted a magical cure.

It had been a long summer, a long, terrible summer. David passed through moments of reality, clinging to scraps of memories that floated by like flotsam. He did this alone. He hated to involve his daughter at this stage. Karen and her husband lived in California in the Bay Area. They had their own lives. He called her often, but he didn't pass on many of the details. He had waited until the middle of July to tell her that he had moved Sarah to the assisted-living home. She was angry for that, but in his defense he didn't want to spoil his daughter's own memories. He had kept these terrible secrets from Karen and tried to hide them in the far back of his own mind. He did this while Sarah fought her own battle, which she lost in some terrible, final way.

He became accustomed to visiting his wife, but now she no longer knew him. She stopped saying his name. The worst thing was she had become angry, almost combative, although there was nothing malicious in her actions because there was no definitive intention to show malice. In an attempt to make her happy, to give her moments of joy, he told her things about Karen and her grandson, Chase. He spoke of their wedding day or the time at Christmas, when he had given Chase a cork gun and Chase had proceeded to shoot all the ornaments on the tree. He brought her a photograph of Karen and she knocked it out of his hands. It clattered on the floor.

And as Sarah lost her memory, he too became lost. He became marginalized, a homeless man in his own home. He felt betrayed by the very existence of his memories, a betrayal of disorder that quietly took away the purpose of them. Every trip down memory lane persisted in tormenting her—and himself. He talked to her about things that no longer meant anything to her, which frustrated him. And when he got home he spent the evenings talking to himself. And it was during the early part of fall, in September, that he remained in this loose, meandering state of contradiction and denial until his daughter called to say she was coming for a visit.

He parked in the cell phone lot just south of the airport terminal, preferring to wait for his daughter's plane to arrive by sitting in a stationary car rather than competing for a spot in a crowded lane encircling the airport. He favored sitting, finding it simpler to not achieve every task, especially at this stage of his life. He had always been active, someone who did a lot of things, someone who made progress in a general forward motion, but Sarah's illness had numbed him, prevented him from wanting to do anything other than just sit. And what else was there to do? Other than her care, there was nothing to pull him along, nothing to propel him into the future. This lack of desire didn't bother him as much as it would have earlier in life, even during these last three years when he was totally motivated to beat Sarah's disease, when their life took a tumultuous turn for the worse.

Karen's plane arrived on time and she called him from the baggage claim area. David pulled up to the curb within minutes and helped put Karen's luggage into the trunk. They got back on the freeway and caught bumper-to-bumper traffic along Lake Washington.

"Why didn't you tell me right away?" asked Karen.

"Things have a way of taking too long," he said.

"Did you think I might have wanted something

else?" she asked.

"It was the right thing to do," said David, after thinking about it a moment. He hadn't worried about Karen's thoughts on this matter.

David checked the car in front of him, a Toyota with only one occupant, and then he honked the horn. "Do I need your permission?" he asked.

"No...."

"Sarah is gone, Karen. She doesn't know me anymore, or her name, or who she is or has been. She doesn't exist anymore in the way you remember."

"I could have helped you through the details."

"Yes, like you were seventeen again," said David. "And we were the perfect father and daughter combo sitting with our coffees while you told me your problems so you could feel better, and so I wouldn't be able to sleep on my own at night thinking about how to solve them for you."

Karen turned her head toward her window.

"Is that how you feel about me?" she asked. "I was a problem for you?"

David sighed, pulling his shoulders down, stretching his neck out. "You know what scares me?" he asked. "You might actually believe it."

Karen didn't speak for a while. They both remained silent until he had turned off the freeway. His house was in the foothills east of Seattle. The last time Karen had been home was four years earlier when Chase was only two and they had flown up to visit during Thanksgiving.

"This week has been the worst for me, an absolute mess," said Karen. "I just feel like I'm going to melt down. Tim doesn't help either. He makes me feel so bad. Every time he opens his mouth, I just want to kill him. He knocks me down with every comment."

"What does he say?"

"He doesn't want me to work," she said. "I don't know why. It's just a part-time job to keep my mind occupied while Chase is in school."

"Keep the job," said David. "Just tell him it's not an option, okay?"

"You don't know Tim," she said. "He has a temper. I don't want to make him mad."

"You're his wife, for Christ's sake," he said.

"He wanted to come up with me, you know," she said. "I wouldn't let him."

David remembered how difficult it was for him to get used to the idea that kids grow up and move away, get married, have children and basically lead their own lives. That they did things their parents didn't know about. And now he didn't want to know everything. He did not want to get pulled into a couple's dispute. He really didn't want to know that his daughter and son-in-law were having problems, although that had not always been the case. He had once wanted to know everything about her, had wanted to keep her safe, but now it was their problem and none of his business.

They pulled into the driveway at the house.

"It looks different," said Karen.

He helped Karen bring her stuff into the house from the car. He put her things in her old room, now the guest room, on the second floor. She began to unpack and he left the room.

"I'll be downstairs," he said. "Are you hungry? I

could put a snack together."

She said no, she didn't want food. She wanted to freshen up.

David was sitting on the sofa in the living room when she came down. The drapes were still closed. He was sitting in the dark.

"This place is like a dungeon," she said, turning on a light.

Karen sat down in a chair opposite him. "How was she this morning?"

David looked at her. She was waiting for an answer he couldn't provide. How could he tell her that he hadn't visited Sarah in the last two weeks? That every time he went he felt sick to his stomach. Why did he have to go it alone? Sarah had been taken from him, leaving him responsible for holding onto all their memories. They had always been together, always inseparable. Where she was now he couldn't go, did not want to go, and so he would miss all that he loved about her. He would miss her humor, the way she smiled, the change in her voice when she was sad. He would regret not being able to sit and hold her hand or know that when she was working in her garden, when she was tinkering in the greenhouse, that she was most happiest. She had made their home special. He couldn't visit her without thinking about what he'd lost. Looking into Sarah's eyes, he couldn't compare anything he saw now with everything he knew about her. She no longer had flowers blooming in her eyes. And in some strange way, he was gone too. He was gone for her, anyway.

No, he couldn't tell Karen that seeing his wife, her mother, made it worse. Each visit added weight to the immense pressure that literally crushed him. His life crumbled apart because there was no one to share it with. Their paths had finally diverted and hers seemed to near an end, arriving at a destination with no purpose, in a place he could not comprehend. Her mind was paralyzed and she was on her way to permanent oblivion. There had been times when he had almost wished that he, too, had moved toward nothingness. But he had had his role to play, and before the incident at the pond, he had told himself he could face each problem as it arose; he could take care of his wife. Despite everything he had been told, he had tried to believe that he could rise above the disease. He had always been a man who did what he should. He was a good employee, a good provider for his family, an active member of their church. He was on the finance board for the Parish School Board. He had done whatever needed to be done, but he couldn't take care of Sarah. The disease was bigger than both of them.

He hadn't realized that he was sitting, staring at the floor. He looked up, alarmed—how long had he drifted?—and saw his daughter in the chair across from him. She was crying, not really looking at him. He knew then he would tell her about the pond. It wasn't right to keep secrets. He would show her where Sarah had trampled the flowers. He would walk her out onto the dock and he would tell her how she had looked and what she had said.

He got up and knelt on the floor in front of her. Seeing his daughter cry dislodged something inside of him. It made a noise in his soul, breaking the quiet disorder in his heart just enough to let in a little bit of light. He could breathe a little better. He said, "Karen, we haven't talked yet, really talked. Let's have some crackers and cheese and a cup of tea, and then we'll go see your mother. I promise. We'll talk along the way. It's going to be difficult, but we'll get through it. You'll see. And later, you can tell me what's going on with you, okay?"

He remained kneeling before his daughter, his only daughter. There was a look of innocence on her face. Her expression warmed and then Karen took his hand and squeezed it so hard it hurt. He didn't know exactly what it meant, he didn't know what she might want from him, but he knew they could talk about it.

Philip came down the steps to the basement and stopped at the bottom of the stairs when he heard voices. He cocked his head. Something about the sounds coming from the other side of the door disturbed him. Was his father really talking to himself? He pushed on the door, gave the room a quick look..

"I heard your voice," said Philip. "Are you alone? I thought someone else was here."

"There should be two of these green tents," his father said, tapping his cane up and down on a green canvas bag.

Philip nodded at once. He managed a smile and took another view of the situation. The important thing right now was to finish helping his father clean the basement and get ready for the move.

"This one's the wall tent, but it's missing the metal poles and iron pegs."

Philip walked over and knelt down by the bag. "Of

course, that's why I put it in the garage sale pile."

"I'm not selling this," said his father, looking down at the tent. "I can make poles out of aluminum tubing."

"But you've got no pegs. And you can't really make them."

"I'll buy new pegs. After this house sells, I'll have enough money to do anything."

"Why not buy another tent?"

"Hell, this tent is practically new. It just needs pegs."

With that Philip stood up. He considered going back home to his wife and family, writing off the morning, but not the whole day. But then he gazed about the room and was reminded of the challenges facing his father. Ten days to move and much to do. Clean the basement and clear out the garage. Yesterday they had worked in the basement to sort things into three different categories: things to keep, things to donate, and things to throw away. Evidently today his father had rearranged the piles.

This didn't surprise him. There was never any reason or motivation on his father's part to follow a plan, and so it was only luck and chance, and help from Philip and his older brother Luis, that any progress had been made shifting through the muddle and chaos of this basement, which was filled with over thirty years of odds and ends. It was an assortment of junk barely worth keeping. Some of it could be donated and the rest would have to be thrown away. There were boxes of silk and wool dresses, pant skirts, summer blouses and an old thermos. A box containing a set of dishes but no cups, gift bags filled with broken toys, greeting cards, an old radio without a dial, a soiled pillow, and a stack of books precariously leaning to one side: *The Way to Dusty Death, Red Fox, The Island, The Haunting of Hill House, As I Lay Dying, Early American Medicine: A Symposium, The Man Within.* A yellow nylon jacket with a broken zipper hung from the rafters. On the wall was a photograph of Mt. St. Helens blowing its top, dark clouds filling the gray sky with rocks, dirt, grass and trees.

Underneath a pile of blankets, Philip found two cane-back chairs, the green velvet cushions crushed and sagging through the worn plywood seat. Perhaps they could be salvaged. You couldn't even sit in them. His mother had bought them at a thrift shop in Sandusky, Ohio. Along with the chairs, he discovered a pair of orange ceramic lamps, a matching set. Their tops curved upward like tulips.

"What's in that box?"

Philip rose from a stooped position. He saw the box his father was pointing at and carried it over, setting it down near his father. His father extended his cane, but the box was just out of reach.

"Damn it," said his father, straining forward. The back of his pants slid down to reveal an ugly scar snaking across his back where white skin puckered up along the row of stitching.

"Why don't you rest?" asked Philip.

His father's body jerked. Behind thick lenses, he rolled his eyes. He wouldn't give up. A bead of sweat hung from his nose, growing larger and larger until it dropped with a plunk on his lap. He ran a red sleeve across his mouth. His disheveled hair gave him the look of someone fresh out of bed. He placed his cane across his knees, moved his wheelchair closer to the box, and managed to hoist it to his lap.

"What's in it?"

"Fishing reels," his father said, pulling one out. It dangled from the end of his outstretched hand. "My single-action fly-casting reel."

Philip wondered about the rod with the cork handle that went along with the reel. His father placed it back in the box and pulled out another reel, a chrome spin-cast, which glinted under the florescent lighting.

"Here," he said, tossing it unexpectedly to Philip.

Philip almost dropped it. It was heavy. "Hey, this is my first reel, the one you gave me on that trip to North Dakota, remember?"

"Thought you might want it."

"Sure, I guess."

Philip inspected it, turning it about, pressing the button on the back to disengage the line pickup. He adjusted the mechanical drag, hearing the clicks and pops as he pulled out the line.

His father closed the flaps on the box, tucking in the edge of each flap until the four corners were secured. "I'm keeping the rest of these," he stammered. "I still fish you know."

He could not believe his father had to remind him. The look of persecution on his father's harassed face stung him sharply. "It's hard to find time," said Philip.

"I've offered to take you out in the boat. You know that."

Philip made a noise, not really a word, to speak in

his defense.

A door closed upstairs. Somebody was in the kitchen, probably Luis getting ready to make lunch. His father took the box and wheeled himself over to the stairs. "I'm going up for another insulin shot."

Philip was the youngest of three sons and whenever he went to visit his father, Luis told Philip all of the things he was doing to keep the old man alive. When Luis talked, Philip listened for what Luis was not telling him. He ignored most of the medical jargon that Luis was becoming quite adept at speaking, the pushing of liquids to keep the kidneys functioning, the constant monitoring of blood pressure, temperature, heart rate, blood sugar, and urine output. Out of respect, he wouldn't disregard any information Luis provided regarding the different types of drugs his father was taking, but he would temper in his own mind the tone in which Luis would recount the facts of dosage, side effects, and possible risks as a person diagnosed with diabetes, high blood pressure and cholesterol, skin rashes and the effects his cancer drug treatment was having on his internal organs.

Many times Luis would speak in front of their father as if he was a patient in a hospital and Luis was his doctor. All of this gave Philip the impression that Luis was doing a considerable job as caretaker, but that he might have forgotten that the patient was in fact their father.

Such was the approach Luis took when it came to preparing their father to move, and when he informed

Philip that he would find a realtor and after appropriate discussion set the asking price, well then Philip could come over and help. Philip asked who would get the house ready and Luis said he would. But they argued anyway. Luis promised him that he would arrange to have someone come in and paint the walls, clean the carpets, and fix the hole in the roof so that the raccoons would have to find somewhere else to live.

So when Saturday had rolled around, the day they would start cleaning, Philip got up early and got dressed. His wife laughed at him when he told her he had to be at his father's house by seven. As he said this, she lifted the covers on the bed. He stared like a teenager at her tanned body. Her smooth, maple bar stomach contrasted with the bright, white cotton. He was unsure as to why she was looking at herself now when she knew he had to go and make sense out of the usual mess that plagued his father. She wasn't malicious, but her smile cut a hole in his stomach. For ten minutes he lay down beside her, fully clothed, while she rolled gently about in beautiful agony, her body arching, as her short breaths and little cries filled the air.

He slipped away from her and found his way downstairs. He let himself out the front door and walked quickly to the car. It began to rain as he backed out of the driveway. He switched on the wipers and that's when he saw Susan, his wife, at the front door, waving, and he smiled.

Susan tolerated his family. Of course she expressed sympathy, but her patience stopped short, especially when it concerned Luis. Susan showed no empathy for his task as a care-giver. She had always said Luis was lazy. And he had lived with his parents for nearly twenty-five years. But Philip realized early enough that Luis was satisfied with his life, and his parents accepted that as much. They were not bothered by this. Philip knew his brother's presence in their home served a purpose. Who else would take care of them? So it didn't bother him, only Susan. Philip never asked her why, but he made up for it by offering to help Luis whenever he needed it. Often it was a medical emergency that brought them all down to the hospital together. Philip let Luis sleep on the worn leather sofa in the waiting area while they waited for the doctor to perform some perfunctory medical treatment that neither made sense nor, after the fact, seemed to do any good.

Eventually, Susan and Philip's interactions with his family settled into a routine that was doable and did not seem to impact the dynamics of their household. It was not the kind of living situation Philip had as a child.

Philip's father traveled a lot when they were kids, spending most of the week on the road, staying at motels and hotels, visiting customers and prospective clients, showing them how to tear down and rebuild hydraulic pumps or transmissions. In his absence, Philip's mother took care of them, did all the work, minded the house, and made sure they did their homework. For that reason she would never be the first to greet him at the front door upon his return. She let him know, through this little act of diffidence, that she didn't like his week-long trips. Their father would never understand and they all knew how their mother felt, but they didn't care, they were just glad that on Friday, usually in the late afternoon or early evening, he'd pull into the driveway. They'd race to the window to look out, to see if he was carrying something extra, a bag or a box. They would wait patiently, the best behavior by far since his departure at the beginning of the week. They waited until he gave them their souvenirs from his trip. Every time. Nothing fancy and never a toy. It was usually a plastic bag filled with trinkets from a trade show or a bar of soap or even matchbooks. Greenbrier Motel of Columbus, Holiday Hotel, The Five Spot, Lacy Lounge, Bob's Big Boy.

On the weekends, to celebrate his coming home, they would go fishing or camping at the state park, pulling the home-built camper behind the car. Once, they owned a two-tone brown and white station wagon. Philip got to sit in the back rear-facing seat. He'd watch the camper trailing behind them, swerving back and forth, and imagine what would happen if the hitch would fail and the safety chains let go, perhaps the moment they rounded a bend on a narrow road going through a mountain pass. The thousand pounds of wood, painted trailer-green, would travel for several feet on its own before the trailer tongue would surrender to the force of gravity, orange and silver sparks flying, metal on asphalt or concrete, and then the steel would buckle, the frame would let go, and the plywood and the two-by-fours would collapse in a gigantic spasm, an explosion of the two summer's worth of hard labor to build it.

Back down in the basement, his father debated the fate of a can of black gun powder. He wanted to give it to Philip, but Philip had no desire to store explosives in his own home. Luis wanted to take it to the dump.

"It's good powder," said Philip's father. "I don't want it to go to waste."

"Maybe we can give it to the local gun range, Pop," said Luis.

"Or sell it," said Philip's father.

"We ain't selling it, Pop," said Luis.

Philip left them arguing and went upstairs to a kitchen filled with dirty dishes. Trash bags lined the wall by the microwave. He walked down the hallway to the bedrooms. In his father's room he noticed that his mother's picture was missing from the wall above the bed. Looking at the faded empty spot he recalled the familiar photograph of her captured in profile, his mother wearing her favorite dress, and her brown hair coiled up in a bun. She had a natural smile back then and the beauty of this particular photograph was how she was bathed in a certain light, a graceful illumination captured in one-one-thousandth of a second. He loved this picture of her, preferring to remember the way she had been before her operation nearly thirty years ago, before the discovery of an aneurysm the size of a lemon in the front, left temporal area of the brain which controlled speech and recognition. This was prior to the weakened artery ballooning out, pressing against her optic nerve and plunging her into temporary darkness. This was back in Ohio on Kent Road in the green Rambler his father had purchased with just twelve hundred dollars down payment.

Then there was his father's transfer to California and the endless trips up the coast to San Francisco to see the neurosurgeon. All this happened during Philip's senior year of high school, a time where false hope and promises discolored the golden sunshine, a time when they trekked across the country in the old Impala, photographing the landscape along the way on Philip's handheld Brownie. His father had bought a new Bell & Howell 8mm movie camera, but he wouldn't let any of the kids use it. Most of the movies showed Philip and Luis standing by some monument or leaning over the wall of a scenic overlook pointing to a rock formation or the gaping hole of the Grand Canyon. Luis had stayed close to their parents even then.

Philip heard Luis coughing in the bathroom. Philip grimaced every time he heard his brother hacking away. His brother's face would turn dark red and Philip guessed one day he would choke or blow an artery. In the living room, Philip located the photograph of his mother on the floor surrounded by other portraits and pictures, each waiting to be packed away into a box for the big moving day. He flipped through them, trying to remember a thing or two about them. He measured the time looking at each by the quality of the memory, by what details he remembered. The charcoal drawings of Japanese waterfowl fascinated him the most. His mother's use of bold color reminded him how close she was to being a professional artist. He smiled. She had been brave enough to hang some of her creations in the hallway, displacing the family vacation pictures, the photo of his father's first deer kill in Pennsylvania, a picture of him sitting in his homemade sailboat in the middle of the Pymatuning Reservoir, and a recent picture of Philip and his wife on vacation in Hawaii.

Luis emerged from the bathroom, victorious once again over excessive mucous and offered to make his lunch. He was going to fix their father a frozen lasagna, but Philip declined.

Their father stopped at the kitchen doorway.

"I hope you're not making lasagna. I'm sick of pasta."

"No," said Luis. "Of course not. This if for Philip."

Philip glanced at his brother, who acknowledged the absurdity of their exchange by grinning at him. Their father shuffled down the hall and Philip heard the bathroom door slam shut.

"He's talking to himself again," said Philip.

"He's having a good day."

"I heard him talking aloud downstairs this morning."

"Where was I?"

"You were up here. I wasn't imagining it, Luis."

"He gets like that when his blood sugar is too low."

Philip disagreed. "I'm worried the cancer might have spread to his brain."

"His brain!" exclaimed Luis. "It's everywhere. Don't you listen? His body scan shows over seventy tumors all over his body. I've mentioned this before. Maybe if you spent more time with him?"

"What's that mean?"

"Come over more often. He likes when you visit."

"I have responsibilities," said Philip.

The microwave buzzer sounded and Luis pulled the cardboard box out, quickly putting it on the counter.

"You do too much," he said. "Too busy for your father."

"Hey," said Philip. "My kids need me."

Luis handed him the lasagna. "Your father needs you too."

The statement meant nothing to him, but the words stayed inside his head. Luis had said it before.

After eating the lasagna, Philip went back down into the basement and soon found himself pawing through another pile in the corner of the basement, back by his father's old desk. He found a canvas bag hanging from a nail behind an old gray coat and carried it over to the desk. Inside the bag he found several tins of old 8mm movies.

"What did you find?"

Philip turned and saw his father rolling his wheelchair across the floor.

"Movies," he said. He handed a film canister to his father. "I think it's our trip to California."

"All right," said his father. "There's a box in the utility closet with the projector. Should be a screen too."

"Where do you want me to put all this?" he asked.

"Get it set up, Philip. Let's watch 'em right now."

"Now?"

"Sure. You're not leaving are you?"

Philip remembered what Luis had said in the

kitchen. "Let's see how much I remember about how to set up the projector."

"Just get it out of the closet," said his father. "I'll set it up. You might break it. They don't make these anymore."

His father threaded the film through the feeder spool. Philip turned the lights out, plunging them into total darkness. The projector shot a beam of white light on to the movie screen. For a moment Philip only saw speckled light, capturing and freezing the particles of dust in the basement. Then he saw himself being chased by Luis across the Great Salt Lake desert. The images moved as if they had a life of their own, a life that existed only on the background of the white movie screen.

His father chuckled. He was smiling and enjoying the moment. Philip didn't know where this was going. An easy flow of music played through the center of his mind as he watched the images of his mother, brother, and father, all playing a part in a movie, dancing about in a lovely, choreographed scene, each destined to act according to their creator. But these were just memories captured on film. These people didn't exist anymore. They were imaginary, remnants from the past.

Philip went home that night feeling like he'd accomplished something. And three days later the three of them convened in the living room, now empty and open. The best it had ever looked in thirty years. It was now a place devoid of all furniture (you could actually see the carpet). Missing were all the things he was used to seeing, the pictures and photos, the stacks of outdoor magazines next to his father's chair, his father's chair, the sofa with its torn arm rest and soiled cushions, the pillows which had been given to his mother by his aunt in Cleveland, the Henley prints of a leopard and a lion above the piano, which was now in his family room waiting to be tuned, and other unusual but familiar items that had made their way into this space his father had called home. Most notably absent was the 10-inch-tall pottery figure of an elderly man smoking a pipe. The old man had stood on the corner of the fireplace mantle since his grandfather had stopped for a visit while on his way to Hawaii.

And then it was time to leave. The three of them crowded by the front door as their father made a big deal out of securing the deadbolt and leaving the keys under the doormat. Philip walked down the steps and waited at the bottom in case their father missed a step or tripped, also wondering what he would do if that ever happened. He had often worried about his father falling down the steps. The walkway was tricky to navigate, but their father used his cane effectively, descending each step until he stood at the bottom of the driveway. Luis positioned the wheelchair behind him and told him to sit.

"That's it boys," said their father, his voice quiet but unwavering as it reflected the importance of the moment. "We got the money. That's all that matters."

"That's right, Pop," said Luis. "Let's go."

Philip hugged his father. "I'll be over at the new

place tomorrow, okay?"

"Sure," said his father. "Just call first, in case we're not home."

"Pop, we don't have phone service yet," said Luis. "It won't be activated until Monday of next week."

Their father nodded. "Then you better not call first. Up to you, Philip."

"We'll probably be asleep in the morning," said Luis. "Come over in the afternoon."

Luis pushed their father down the sidewalk to their car. One man standing. One man sitting. Missing was their mother. Philip watched Luis open the car door and when he offered assistance to their father, he refused to have Luis help him, even pushed his arm away. That single gesture revealed itself clearly. Philip imagined his father knew all along, once Mom had passed away before him, knew that he would bury her at the National Cemetery, knew that he wouldn't be much further behind. He was just preparing to go. And leaving now gave him authority, a sense of control. He had chosen his own method of departure.

Philip sat in the front seat of his truck, holding the spinning reel in his hands. The metal was cold, hard. He turned the crank. It was as smooth as the day he pulled it new from a box. He watched them drive by. He waved, neither of them waved back, their focus on the road ahead. Their brake lights flashed once as their car came to a stop at the corner. Luis would take the long route to the new place, a road that was narrow and would lead them through the undeveloped parts of the county. But it was the quickest way there. Philip didn't give much thought to the time of day, even though it was late. When it got dark, after the sun had dipped below the edge of the mountains to the west, shadows would fall across the road and make it difficult to see, making it too dangerous to drive or to navigate if you were tired or old or in pain.

This road, thought Philip, where would it take his father? How much longer would he be traveling on it? Perhaps, he thought, it would take him down the back roads of hell or even heaven. And would Philip's mother be waiting for him at the door? Philip pulled the truck away from the curb, heading home. He felt both shame and pride after watching Luis and their father drive away. Shame for not spending more time with them, but glad for the time he had spent helping them prepare to move on. The weather had turned dark and as he came down the hill, he held tightly onto the steering wheel. His thoughts turned away from the gray sky to the image of a day in summer, warm enough to take the boat out into the lake, or to take a solitary walk on the beach where footprints left in the sand would capture small amounts of water and turn into real feet, or spend an evening at the local ice creamery, sitting on a picnic table holding onto single dip cones, watching the kids climb on top the cow and rock it back and forth on its cheap wooden wheels. He imagined all of this before turning onto the freeway.

DOUBLE BUBBLE

Twenty minutes he sits in the car watching the door. He could've been in and out in ten minutes or less. He reaches into his shirt pocket and pulls out a pack of gum. He is never without gum, not since he gave up smoking. He jams a stick in his mouth and launches the foil wrapper out the window with a flick of his thumb just as a young guy in a tan shirt and black apron passes by pushing a line of shopping carts. He looks at him. Like he is going to get out and pick up the paper.

Two teenage girls walk past, talking and laughing. He watches their butts. Both are dressed in green and white sweatpants and sweatshirts. School colors, he thinks. The one on the left with sunglasses pushed back into her long, blonde hair is more attractive. He would dislike the other. Her neck glistens in the sunlight. Is it sweat? He wonders if she just finished a jog. She probably smells right now.

Twenty-seven minutes and she is still in the

grocery store. She will stay in there forever. They had argued over something stupid, like where to go today. She had plans, but he wanted to take a drive. She yelled and then he yelled. It went on like that for several minutes before she gave in. She told him they'd have to go to the store first. She wanted a picnic lunch. Now he feels bad for yelling at her and thinks he knows why he gets so angry and what makes him want to go at her. She talks loud that much he knows. Time after time he tells her to lower her voice. She never listens, just speaks louder like she hasn't heard him or doesn't want to hear.

She comes strolling out of the store like she'd only been gone for a few minutes. He rolls the window up and turns on the radio. He finds a station real quick and raises the volume. It is blasting when she opens her door. She squeezes in with two bags on her lap. She doesn't bother with the seat belt. Maybe taking a ride isn't such a good idea, he thinks.

He crosses the intersection and drives down the hill towards the lake and glimpses a speck of sunlight in the clouds overhead. At the bottom of the hill he turns right, passing an old man walking alongside the road where he used to jog a couple miles each day. There are too many distractions now to even think about exercise, and he looks briefly in the mirror, seeing the man stumble and then regain himself. With so many cars now on the road, he hopes the man's life will not be complicated by taking time for a walk. He would hate to read about a man lying dead on the road.

The beach area at the lake is deserted. He parks the car in the handicapped spot. She glances at him, but says nothing. She gets out and walks away from the car, carrying the two bags, but he can't tell where she is going to sit. Picnic tables are still stacked on end by a maintenance shed. A small flock of geese stand around a muddy puddle. He follows her and they end up sitting on a bench by the walking trail. From one of the grocery bags she pulls out a beer and gives it to him. He tries chugging it all in one gulp, beer spilling down each corner of his mouth. She shakes her head, eyes closing briefly like she's put off by something he did. He burps and then wipes the back of hand on his forehead. He's been hot all day. He looks at the lake and thinks how cool it would be to jump in. He tells her this. She dares him to jump in. Without thinking, he runs straight for the water until he is up to his knees, and he is shouting it is so cold, and then he dives head first, vanishing down under the water. He stays down until his lungs are screaming and then he comes up for air.

"Are you crazy?" she yells.

"Yes."

"Come out, you're wet."

"Cold, too," he says. He crosses his arms.

"Here," she says, handing him her coat. "Wrap yourself up."

He does and it helps. They sit down on the bench. They are together, he thinks. This is what matters. He spits out his gum before kissing her on the mouth. She pulls away. She grabs the second grocery bag and lifts out a plastic tub. She holds it up for him to see.

"Angel food cake," she says.

"What's the expiration date?" he asks. "Is it expired? You know I hate expired food."

She raises her eyebrows, but turns the plastic tub around until she can read the label.

"Well?"

"Says tomorrow's date."

"Let's eat it."

She hands him the tub. He opens the lid and breaks off a chunk of angel food. That's when he notices she is walking back to the car.

"Where you going?"

"Eat your cake," she says.

He watches her get into the car. She's mad again. Get over it, he thinks. But he isn't worried. She'll calm down later. She'll think about things and then everything will be all right. Things always turn out right. Always. He looks at her and she waves at him. See, he knows all about her. He smiles and then just as he waves to her he sees the car move backwards. He jumps up. Hey! She almost hits the tree behind her and then she is moving forward, tearing through the gravel parking lot and then she is gone.

"Where you going?" he yells. He looks around, but he is all alone in the park. Even the geese by the utility shed have wandered off. He makes up his mind to wait. She'll be back. Yes, he knows all about her. She'll come back for him once she gives it some thought. After she calms down and realizes things always turn out right. Always.

He eats the rest of the cake, but he has nothing to wash it down with. His beer is gone. He gets up and walks around the park looking for a drinking fountain. Nothing. He goes back to the bench and gives the bags a second look, but there is nothing but the plastic tub. He feels a stickiness to the bottom of the plastic. He flips it over and notices the orange sticker, a sale sticker. Angel food cake for half price. He looks at the date on the label. The cake expired two days ago. She lied to him.

He starts to feel funny. Is it the cake? He needs a drink. He looks at the lake for no reason. That gets him thinking about his gum. He tosses the plastic tub and gets down on his hands and knees looking for his gum. God, he hopes he didn't spit it into the water. He had kissed her right on the bench. He looks under the bench and then he starts looking in the grass. He is never without gum.

"Tell me about your mother. Tell me about her relationship with your father."

"They didn't have relations," she says.

"Of course they did," he says. "They had you."

"That doesn't mean they loved each other."

"Well, it meant they liked each other enough to have sex, unless you were adopted."

"I wasn't adopted."

"They were married when they had you?"

"Of course they were."

"Were they trying to get pregnant?"

"I don't know that. And I never asked them."

"It matters," he says. "Maybe they used contraceptives that were defective? Maybe the rubbers were past expiration?"

She turns away, pulling the covers off of him. He pulls them back, leaving her body partially uncovered. He stares at her shoulders, the strands of blonde hair, and her bra straps. She begins to laugh.

"What's so funny?"

"I never thought of my parents as lovers."

"Why?"

"They rarely kissed each other in public."

"Or held hands?"

She frowns. "Does holding hands constitute a relationship?"

"Yes," he says. "Are you worried about us holding hands?"

She turns back, adjusting the pillow so she can see him.

"I don't mind," she says, putting her hand out.

He takes it. Her fingers are long and thin. She has tiny fingernails, painted pink.

He starts tracing the veins on the back of her hand, rubbing tiny circles with his finger along her wrist, gradually moving his hand up her arm to her shoulder.

"So they never held hands?"

"My parents hardly occupied the same room," she says. "My mother lived her whole life in the kitchen. She baked."

"So she cooked for him?"

"What kind of question is that? She cooked all the meals."

"What was her specialty? Burgers? Steak? Shrimp Scampi?"

She pulls her hand away and leans it against her forehead. A tiny noise escapes from her lips, like she just uncovered a faint memory.

"I'd forgotten about her pastries," she says. "Pies and tarts."

"What kind of pie?"

"Pecan, apple, strawberry."

"Strawberry's good."

"I remember helping her bake strawberry pie for someone's birthday. I stood on this little stepstool by the sink and washed the berries. I could barely reach the faucet. The plump red strawberries were as big as my fist. I really enjoyed mashing them in the bowl with a fork. My mother would measure out just the right amount of sugar. Sometimes she'd use cornstarch, but I always asked for sugar. Then she'd boil the mixture on the stove until it was a glaze. She would pour that on top of the pie crust and the fresh strawberries."

"Sounds delicious. God, I'm hungry."

"It was like liquid candied apples or sweet, red maple syrup. The pie looked so good I didn't want to cut into it. It was so perfect. Something we had done together."

"Who baked pies after she died?"

"No one," she says.

He leans up on one elbow.

"I'll make you a pie," he says. "Today."

"Sure."

"Really. Strawberry pie with whipped cream."

"You're crazy."

"No, I'm just a pie lover."

She is quiet for a while.

"I don't want any pie."

"You're doing it again," he says.

"Doing what?"

"Not letting yourself have any fun."

"Well, I don't feel happy anymore," she says. She leaves the bed and disappears into the bathroom, closing the door behind her.

He follows and listens by the door. She is crying. He knocks softly.

"Go away. I'm taking a bath."

He knocks again. "I'll have the pie ready when you're done."

She turns on the water for the tub.

"You don't even have strawberries," she says.

"I'll grow them and by the time you finish soaking they'll be plucked and boiling on the stove. I'll be sure to use sugar."

He listens until the water stops running. He imagines her immersed under a voluminous cloud of bubbles, like foam on a root beer float, only white. He pulls on his jeans and a shirt. He stands in front of the mirror and combs his hair. He goes downstairs to the kitchen and finds his pack of gum on the counter by his car keys. He pops a stick in his mouth. Then he has an idea. Before opening the door on the refrigerator, he prays for strawberries.

"When do you want to go out again?"

"No more parties," she says.

"A movie with popcorn."

"No dinner?"

"Sure, but not Dutch. I'll pay for the meal, the movie tickets, the popcorn and all the pop you can drink. I'll pay for everything, but only if you read some more poetry."

"I'm not a poet."

"Then I'm not paying."

She's silent, pondering. He sees her shift instinctively into thinking about a poem. He knows her. She'll speak soon.

Finally she says, "Here's one."

He smiles.

You ask what tempts me most.
On wings my mind flees in fright,
Before taste swallows apple seed.
What you see is a ruse to touch my own breast.
Here, the world is playfully calling.
Rise, quickly and in earnest.
Forget these trite musings
And ask me no more.

"There," he says. "With that you're already paid up. Tomorrow night?"

"You're nuts."

She gives him a drink and he tastes it. The frozen taste of mint and cherry sticks to his lips. He realizes that the cherry part is a piece of paper. He flicks it on the floor. The drink allows him to see the smallest things. The piece of lint on the jacket of his coat. A speck of black inside the folded tissue of a single tulip in the vase on the other side of the room, bathed underneath the glow of a single overhead light bulb.

She sits next to him on a round cushion. Someone has taken a chisel and carved dark slits under both eyes. Her pupils are as large as cat's eyes. He almost freaks when she opens her mouth and a clear white liquid spills out onto her lower lip and dribbles down onto her blouse. She licks her lips. Did she just do that?

This is what life brings. Unexplained craziness.

She needs fresh air and he leads her by the arm through the house to the front door. They step out onto the porch. She pulls away when a car drives by honking its horn. She stumbles on the bottom steps and falls into the bushes. He pulls her to her feet.

"What are you doing?"

"Leave me be," she says.

"I won't until you talk."

"Nothing to say."

"Sure you do. Everyone has something to say."

"I set aside everything I ever want to share with anyone."

That stops him. "Beautiful," he says. "Pure poetry."

"Huh?"

"A line like that is simple, clean and uncluttered."

"You're just saying that."

"Tell me," he says, "What did you set aside?"

"Me."

"Yeah."

"Why did you bring me here?" she asks.

"You looked lost back there."

"I still am," she says. "Haven't you figured that out? I'm empty."

"But not abandoned."

She looks from side to side.

"Where's my purse?"

"It's gone."

He takes her back inside and they sit by the

fireplace.

She wants something to wipe her face.

He gets up and brings her back a handful of paper napkins. She takes one and blows her nose. She wipes the corner of her mouth and then her eyes. She succeeds in streaking her makeup.

"Here," he says. "Let me help."

He wets the napkin and works at rubbing off the black grease from underneath her eyelid. The fire is warming her. Her hands stop shaking. It looks like a piece of her soul is starting to wake up.

"What did you like about it?" she says.

"The line?" he asks, guessing.

She nods.

"It moved me and made me wonder, you know, about you. Could you say it for me?"

She thinks for a moment, wanting to get it right for him.

"I set aside everything I ever want to share with anyone."

He asks her to go to a movie. He finds out she lives in an apartment along the lake. After the movie they eat breakfast at a pancake place. They plan another night out together. He suggests a party.

He is never without gum, so when he stops to get gas the cashier is chewing a big wad. She blows a big bubble right in front of him.

"I could use some of that," he says.

She blows another bubble.

He pays for the gas and asks for her phone number.

She gives him her number and a pack of Double Bubble.

LITTLE FLOWER,
LITTLE SPARROW

He collapsed at the shop of Pierre Chatellier after inspecting the rows of miniature puffs, éclairs and tarts which looked like comical eyeballs laid out neatly on a pan. He was up righted and flung down on the floor by several sharp pains in his chest. There was a single moment in which he wanted to leave his body, to pull free from the carcass of bone and withered flesh. Already his image in the polished glass of the display case reminded him of the recent wrestling match he'd seen on television, a much advertised debacle between the Greek Tragos and the Norwegian Dusik. The match lasted only five minutes before Tragos broke Dusik's back after flipping him over his head into the corner rails.

The shop's proprietor rushed over, muttering excuses under his breath and pulled him to his feet. He pointed Louie to the front door and told him to get out. Louie stuck out his tongue and left the store as though he was no longer interested in spending his money there.

He didn't know what to do next, thinking he must be an idiot for creating a scene. And though the ache in his chest had subsided, he hoped he hadn't used up all of his luck. Outside he looked up and down the sidewalk. He would walk along the Café de la Paix among the crowds of excited youths and women, but taking steps proved difficult. He managed to place one foot in front of the other, moving slowly enough to remember what it was like to crawl on his knees as a child.

Louie understood what it meant to be sick, and to be an old fool, a fraud. He would not change his habits, though, and when he spotted a woman with a large bag strolling along the rue Auber he summoned more courage and trotted across the wet pavement. He situated himself at a convenient distance behind her. She was a leisurely type, aimlessly wandering in and out of shops, searching for a gift or simply wanting to look at things. When she entered a clean, well-lit store that sold kitchen and bathroom items, he stood near the entrance and studied the white and yellow ceramic dishes in the window. He was reminded that his were both cheap and ugly.

She did not come out as soon as he would have liked. He wasn't in so much of a hurry, but already the morning light had shortened the shadows and brightened doorways and alleys. If he were to do something today it would have to be soon. Earlier that morning, when it was easier to find a target among those waiting for the trains at the Gare de Lyon, he had tried to relieve a gentleman of his briefcase, but the lights had gone up all at once along the platform as the train arrived, appearing from the cold breath of darkness along the rails.

In a little while he would leave her, make his way home. He was feeling better now and he had his spring back in his step. Things would go on. Life would go on. He was relieved when she reappeared, passing by close enough for him to catch the scent of summer and autumn flowers, sumac roses and oeillets, evoking a childhood memory… a village near Giverny, a gothic church, fields of red perennials. As he let himself get lost in this thought, he became aware that she was getting away. He stuffed the memory away and began walking in earnest. He quickly caught up to her.

When she entered a side street onto the Boulevard Des Capucines, the sidewalk was busy, a lot of people coming and going, and he considered grabbing her purse and disappearing into the crowd. Already the physical act of stealing played through his mind. He would yank at the strap on her shoulder and then run as fast as he could down the street and hope to disappear along the garden walls of the Convent. Many times he had crouched on the other side of the brick wall, hidden from sight by overgrowing clusters of trees and bushes, ravaging the interior compartments of a Louis Vuitton.

When she reached a spot along the street where the sunlight was interrupted by the façade of a tall building, he started to sprint, quietly on his toes. She was wearing heels; he wore his flat shoes, which were to his advantage. Then it was time to act. He was just about to reach for the bag when she turned abruptly into the doorway of a café. What luck for her! He had to slip by and continue running, stopping only when he was sure no one had seen his attempt. He strolled back and walked slowly past the Café's open doorway. Through the darkness he thought he saw her take a seat at the bar near the back wall.

He wandered up and down the Boulevard Des Capucines, but kept coming back to the Café and each time he did she was still sitting, and the more he saw her alone without company the more he became interested and the more he wanted to know why she sat alone drinking. She did not look like a woman accustomed to loneliness, so who was she? Why did she come here and why did she stay so late? These questions plagued him and a new plan began to form in his mind, one that would require the boldness of the direct approach.

"You've been watching me. Have we met before?"

"Perhaps," he said, wanting everything in the world to be right. "You look familiar."

By his second drink, it was becoming clear that the woman before him looked familiar. She reminded him of someone from his past, a vague memory that confused him, and it was not until she took a cigarette from her purse and tapped it three times on the palm of her hand that he remembered her name. Edith.

He ordered another glass and quickly swallowed, letting the rush of liquid burn the back of his throat. He stood up with the intention of asking for her name, to confirm his suspicion that she was Edith. He approached cautiously, his legs shaking either from doubt or from the second glass of brandy. What if he was wrong and this woman was not Edith? Would she even want to talk with him? And if he were mistaken – but how could he? He had seen the same gesture years ago, so it was not possible she was someone else - then he would apologize for his intrusion and return to his table where he was sure his half bowl of peanuts would be waiting.

He sat down next to her and before he could speak she turned her head to stare at her own reflection in the mirror. They locked eyes briefly as they both saw her dark auburn curls which covered the left side of her face and shoulder and in his estimation made the right side even more beautiful.

"Yes," she said, "that is me."

Edith would have spoken like this, a hint of humor and absurdity to be lavished on her admirer. He found his heart beating faster.

"Tell me your name," she said, returning her gaze to the drink in the glass.

"Louie."

"Ah, a name that I shall never forget."

"Really?"

She amused herself by laughing a little. "A different Louie," she said. "He's dead."

"I'm sorry."

"Please don't be apologetic. It is better that he died."

He placed his hands in his lap, squeezing them together, pinching his finger. "Oh, then I must tell you that I feel quite sure that you are someone I know."

"Really?"

"Yes."

"You'll have to excuse me. I am not used to being picked up in a place like this."

"Picked up?"

"You are trying to get to know me, maybe even get my phone number, or address, to speak with me and send me flowers?"

"No, no. That is not it," he said. He lifted a hand to his forehead to rub a spot on his skin that was starting to ache.

"Oh, I see," she said. "You wish more from me. Do I look that easy?" She turned towards her reflection once again. "Yes, I can see how you have confused me for someone else, someone in a different profession I think."

"You might be a little drunk," he said. "I'm not here to pay for your company."

"Then you must want payment from me?" she asked. Her lips curved down, not from sadness, but from circumspection as she looked him over. "A decent coat and shoes. Give me your hands."

"My hands?"

"Yes, I want to see the palms of your hands, to see the lines that will tell me if you are worth something."

He didn't give her his hands. "Please," he asked quickly. "Tell me, is your name Edith?"

"Yes, I am Edith."

Edith. Astonished that it was that simple, he sat back as a little of the earlier tension gave way to recognition and affirmation.

But then she turned slightly in her chair, leaning towards him. "I can be your Edith, your Lauren, even your sister if you would like."

It occurred to him that she had just mocked him,

twisting his question the way one would spin yarn around a finger. He found it difficult to concentrate and had the impression she was playing a game. There could be no mistake now. She was Edith.

He raised a finger to the bartender and asked for a drink.

"I see that I upset you," she said. She touched his arm with her hand. "Please, I apologize."

"It's okay," he said.

Then she stood up, pulling her coat over her shoulders. "Let's go," she said emphatically. "I have a place over on Montmartre near the Musée Grévin. We could walk and talk along the way. You can ask me many questions."

He was seized by her manner, by her wild beauty, an abrupt contrast to his own life. She nudged him playfully as they left the Café, pulling on his arm as though they had a common bond of friendship, or more. He bloomed from this new feeling, no longer old and desperate.

"Louie, have you seen the changes at Grévin?"

He shrugged. "I have not been inside the wax museum for some time."

"They have redone Jeanne d'Arc burning at the stake," she said, almost whispering it in his ear. "You must see it."

"Oh, I don't think that it's necessary."

"Louie, you must. I insist," she said, pulling on his arm again.

They left the Boulevard Des Capucines and were now nearing the corner of Montmartre. He couldn't help wondering at her sudden obsession with the wax figures.

"Here it is," she said, dragging him to the museum's entrance.

Many times he had walked by this spot without ever looking up, but now he stood on his heels outside 10 Boulevard Montmartre, gazing up past the arched, rose-colored marble entrance, seeing the large gold letters announcing Musée Grévin, the Cabinet Fantastique and the Palaise des Mirages. He realized that she was indulging herself in some way that he couldn't understand. Perhaps it was just an experiment to defeat boredom. But by her side, for whatever reason other than his own curiosity, he no longer had the sense of isolation, of being alone, which had come too quickly for him in life. He paid the 65 francs, and Edith pushed him inside towards Famous Figures to see the wax replicas of the world's greatest inventors, artists and philosophers. She said, "Louie, whom do you like best?"

There were so many. Da Vinci. Renoir. Voltaire. Others. He couldn't decide.

"The light is patchy, artificial," he said, "but Leonardo looks so regal. His posture, his complexion and expression, the white beard, strong hands. I wish I had his nose. It is so prominent."

"He's one of my favorites too."

"Yes," he said, wishing for a moment that he could be sitting there at this desk with a pen in his left hand, his right hand holding some sort of object, perhaps one of his inventions, a working model or prototype, while the young boy at his side gazed at him with large eyes, a wide smile consuming the entire lower half of the child's face. The boy's happiness brought a smile to his own face and Edith took his arm and gripped it tight. They strolled past other exhibits and in the section called Artisans, Edith read from one of the information cards located in front of a display of famous painters. Louie was astonished to learn that Édouard Manet was not Claude Monet and that Manet had painted *The Luncheon on the Grass* instead of Renoir who had painted *Luncheon of the Boating Party*, and that Monet was the one who painted water lilies.

It took almost two hours to see the entire museum and they spent an extra few moments gazing at multiple reflections of themselves along the rows of mirrors. On their way to her place further down Montmartre they strolled through a park where they stood at the edge of a wide, expansive grass lawn which had opened up and allowed them to see north towards the hill of Montmartre. Edith pointed and Louie could barely discern the white-domed Basilique du Sacré Cœur on its summit. But then she tugged at him to follow her in the opposite direction, and his enthusiasm diminished when he thought she was leading him to Pigalle and the plaza of sex shops on the main boulevard. In time, though, he saw they were not going that way.

At one point she started walking ahead of him, almost at a run and it surprised him. She stopped to allow him to catch up and when he did she adopted a long brooding look.

"Where are we going?" he demanded.

"To my place, remember?"

They were standing underneath the glow of a streetlight.

"Who are you?"

She laughed and it crossed his mind that she was someone like him, but then she grabbed his hand and gave it a squeeze. He knew she wasn't the same Edith he had met before, but in a voice that sounded like church bells ringing, she said, "Follow me."

They walked on Montmartre until the darkness covered them entirely.

THE HAPPY COUPLE

I have to put up with some things just to be with Trudy. Like she can't see too well, so when she drives I have to clench my fists and hope to God that she don't kill us. Of course when I'm behind the wheel she's telling me how to drive.

There's other things. Her idea of breakfast is yogurt. Dinner is always out. Like we have time to eat together anyway, she works so much. She's happiest when she's selling makeup. Trudy has a mobile salon and manicure business and makes good money. She listens to her customers. Just the other day she opens a box and pulls out three tubes of lipstick. She shoves a tube underneath my nose. Smell it, she says.

It smells like cardboard. "You sure about these?"

She hands me another. "That one's Plum Vogue."

"Smells sweet," I say. "Like you."

"One more," she says.

I have to smell it twice. "Reminds me of your sister."

"My sister?"

"Yeah, after she's been breastfeeding her kid. What's it called?"

"Baby Sweetheart."

"Women will go for that," I say.

She has this same box balanced on her lap as we careen around the next corner. We're headed north on our way to Magnolia and Trudy's letting me drive her car. We agreed that I'd drive as long as we get to her next appointment by nine o'clock. Trudy found this place by accident. She calls it her little gold mine. The Sunset Memorial Retirement Home is a two story building, L-shaped, set back in the trees in the shadow of a hill. All the rooms are painted in drab yellows and greens. It's certainly not my idea of retirement.

"Good, you're here," says Andre, the manager at Sunset. He walks us through the lobby. "I've got you in the cafeteria annex. Three tables, right?"

"Thanks, hon," says Trudy. "And I'm going to need that portable sink. Mrs. Lewis is getting her hair done today."

Trudy's business has grown to three tables now that she sells a complete line of cosmetics. She has products for the eyes, lips and face, makeup removers, brushes, sponges and pads, even travel mirrors. Recently she started to sell body and bath products. Shimmers, powders, and body bronzers.

Mrs. Lewis arrives and waltzes right past Trudy. She reaches out to give me a hug.

"There's my young man," she says, clutching me in her arms.

"Hey, babe."

Mrs. Lewis laughs. "Trudy, you should marry this one. He's cute."

I help put Mrs. Lewis in the chair. "What color are we doing today?"

"Red," she says, her lips smacking together.

Mrs. Lewis winks at me and I wink back. She likes the attention. Her first husband died back in Michigan. They lived in Sault Ste. Marie on the Upper Peninsula. After her husband's death, Mrs. Lewis came out west to visit her brand new baby granddaughter. Now she's here at Sunset and remarried.

Right behind Mrs. Lewis is Mr. Lewis, being pushed by Rhoda, a volunteer who helps bring the residents down the hall from their rooms when its time. Trudy thinks Rhoda likes me. I tell her she's too old.

Rhoda pushes Jack's wheelchair into a corner and spins him around. I wave a hand in front of his face. "Hey Jack!" Rhoda adjusts the bib around his neck so he doesn't drool on his shirt. Rhoda thinks Jack enjoys watching his wife get her hair done. Since he never smiles I don't know how she has this belief. Jack's eyes are glazed over like jelly donuts.

Trudy helps Mrs. Lewis into a chair in front of the portable sink. While Trudy washes her hair, I squeeze several puffs of baby powder on her arms and rub them. Then while Trudy starts cutting her hair Rhoda takes me to the kitchen to fetch a plate of brownies.

"I see you here all the time," she says.

"Good business for Trudy," I say. "I think today she'll sell out of the Ruby Red."

"She counts on you to help."

"She would do as good on her own," I say.

Rhoda narrows her eyes.

"What?" I ask.

"Just wondering," she says. "About you and Trudy."

"Me and Trudy."

"As a couple."

"A couple of what?"

She sighs. "Listen, Carl. Do you love her?"

"You're serious, aren't you?"

"Yeah," she says.

This is one of those times where I'm expected to say something glib or corny, but Rhoda isn't in one of her kidding around moods. There's something different in the way she talks, the way she looks.

Rhoda was getting me thinking. I can be an hour away on my own and I'll get these images of Trudy that make me happy. There's one I especially like of Trudy sitting in our bed on top of the sheets. She's wearing a white camisole with spaghetti straps. She's got one leg folded underneath her body and she's leaning her elbow on top of the knee on her other leg which is bent. Her legs are like honey, all smooth and sweet.

Rhoda grabs a bag of chips from the counter. She hands them to me.

"Here," she says. "For when you get hungry later."

Mrs. Lewis is done getting her hair colored and it's ready to dry. I pull her up to her feet and steady her while Trudy positions the dryer behind her chair.

When her eighty-three-year-old head is covered by a glowing dome of iridescent coils Mrs. Lewis pinches my arm and reveals a mouth full of mucous. I was sure her teeth were going to fall out. I just pat her on the shoulder and take a step backwards. I still have bruises on my arm from the last time we were here. Not all were from Mrs. Lewis. Many of Trudy's customers are older women like Mrs. Lewis who need the benefits of a perm. They need other benefits too, and sometimes the women of Sunset stop me in the hall, grasping my arm, giving it a good squeeze. They each have their own special way of saying it, but the message is the same. My husband was good, but he's dead now. You're a fine looking young man. Busy tonight? I detest the thought of growing old. Everything wrong with them is due to their age. Sometimes I shove a finger in my mouth, gagging myself, just as an older lady turns away and Trudy knows she must have said something colorful.

The women of Sunset are generous today and the Red Ruby sells out. Trudy and I take a break, digging into the bag of chips Rhoda gave me. I pull Trudy into my arms and give her a quick kiss, which lasts longer than it should. Trudy gives a look at Mr. Lewis in the chair next to us. The smile on his face is not from our display of love.

"Will we act like this at their age?" I ask.

"Only I don't want you talking as much as Jack here," says Trudy.

"Listen," I say. "We ain't going to do much talking. We'll be too busy."

"Doing what?"

"You know."

"I can guess."

"Marry me and I'll tell you. Otherwise it's a secret."

"Did you just propose to me?"

"Maybe," I say.

"Hmm." Trudy puts her hand out like she's admiring a ring on her finger.

"You did propose, didn't you?"

Trudy leans against me and we stay close like that for a moment, hugging, until Mrs. Lewis starts in on a phlegm attack. With her head shoved inside the hair dryer and wrapped in a thick layer of rollers, she shakes like a ten-year-old Whirlpool out of balance. "You still in there?" I yell, rapping the dryer with my knuckles. Mrs. Lewis can't hear me. I look at Trudy, who is giving me a searing look, very subtle, but I see it anyhow, tucked away in the corner of her lips. Mrs. Lewis sounds worse. "Better get the money now."

Trudy's parents are not the best pick either. Her mother, Mrs. Gunther, is Catholic so we spend Sunday mornings driving her to Our Lady of Perpetual Help. When Mass is over we take Mrs. Gunther out to eat lunch and by the time we get her home she's ready for bed. I try to picture her sitting in one of those drab yellow rooms at Sunset.

Her husband, Ed, is all right. He puts up with stuff too, I'm sure.

They're surprised to see me without Trudy. My timing is all off. Ed is in the middle of wrestling and he's cheering on The Undertaker. I think I catch both of them off guard with my question. Mrs. Gunther tells me to sit down so we can talk.

"So many young people think they're in love," says Mrs. Gunther.

"We are in love," I say.

"But how do you know?"

"I just know."

"That's only part of the equation," she says.

"Trudy loves me too."

Mrs. Gunther cranes her neck up and to the right, looking at her husband. "Tell him Ed," she says. "Tell him it's not that easy. "

Ed grunts. "It's not that easy."

"Of course, you can't really tell if you love someone or not until you've known that person for awhile. Love doesn't happen overnight, Carl. "

Mrs. Gunther emphasizes the overnight part, inferring something I'm not sure I want to discuss.

"We're getting married, Mrs. Lewis. I wanted your permission."

Mrs. Gunther rises from the sofa. She shuffles to the chair her husband sits in. "Turn that thing off," she says.

Ed curses under his breath. He mutes the television instead of turning it off. He swivels around to face me. "Why'd you go ahead and ask our permission? Trudy is old enough to make up her own mind. If you loved her, you woulda known this."

Mrs. Gunther stares at me suspiciously. "You must've known we wouldn't go easy. Her older sister got married and divorced twice from the same person. Some fool from Alabama who's only interest, mind you, was sex."

Ed laughs.

"What's so funny?" asks Mrs. Gunther.

"I can't imagine Lois having sex with Leslie. He was shorter than her and he smelled like bluegill."

"He worked at a restaurant, Ed. You get smells working at a restaurant."

"I know what bluegill smells like. I don't know any restaurant that serves bluegill from here down to Eugene."

"All right, enough," says Mrs. Gunther. "I was trying to make an analogy so Carl would understand."

"Oh, I understand, Mrs. Gunther." I say.

She brightens. "You do?"

"Yes. You don't want me to marry Trudy just for sex."

She reddens.

"I appreciate your candor, young man," says Ed. He is leaning over on his knees. His aren't skinny at all and the biceps in his arm are suddenly bulging. "But I get funny when someone mentions my daughter's name and the word sex in the same sentence."

"But you just did," I say.

He smiles. "Someone other than me."

"I simply meant that sex is sex, but love is something different."

Mrs. Gunther is silent, then she says, "What is it then?"

I say, "It's more than sex."

"Carl."

Ed's leaning forward again.

They're waiting for me to talk. My heart is pounding. I try to think about why I love Trudy. She's wonderful of course, but that wouldn't do. No, Mrs. Gunther needs convincing. I think about all of Trudy's good traits, but before I can speak to them the front door opens and in walks Trudy.

"Hey, all," she says.

Thank God. I give her a quick thumbs down. She frowns.

Ed stands up and so does Mrs. Gunther.

Trudy gives each a hug and then grabs my hand.

"We're going out to celebrate," she says.

Mrs. Gunther surprises all of us by walking to the kitchen. "I can fix dinner if you don't mind fish sticks."

Trudy looks at me. We never eat at her parents.

"Let's celebrate," she says.

"Celebrate what?" I ask.

"Us," she says. "Let's eat downtown tonight, okay?"

Mrs. Gunther yells from the kitchen. "I got chicken from yesterday I can cook."

Trudy rushes into the kitchen after her. "Mama, Carl's taking me to a nice restaurant."

By then both Ed and I are in the tiny kitchen as well.

"Why? You can eat here. It's no problem."

"You know why, Mama," she says. "To celebrate."

Mrs. Gunther says nothing, but then Ed comes to everyone's rescue.

"Trudy deserves a nice meal," he says, putting an arm around his wife. He turns to Trudy. "Make sure he buys all three meals. Breakfast, lunch and dinner."

Yeah, I put up with some things just to be with Trudy.

NECESSARY SIN

At the urgent care clinic Domingo held her brother Theo's hand. Color from his blue blanket leeched onto his lips. He was shivering. Domingo leaned into her mother's shoulder, trying to keep away from the man sitting next to her. He had a bloody rag wrapped around his forearm near the wrist. Her mother had this faraway look in her eyes. Something washed over her pupils.

A nurse summoned them. Her mother cradled Theo in her arms and they followed the nurse to Room 28. They put Theo into a bed. The nurse positioned Theo's head on a soft pillow. She pressed a button and the bed moved up with an electric hum. She drew blood and soon his arms were laced with tubes. Bags hung above him, dripping glucose into his vein. A young doctor appeared holding an x-ray film. He talked about a hip fracture before the nurse grabbed his arm, whispering into his ear that he had the wrong patient. He smiled before turning away.

The nurse told her mother that they would have to do a full workup on Theo before the doctors knew anything.

The nurse looked at Domingo. "Please wait in the other room," she said.

Domingo wandered down a corridor, looking into each room. Men with big bellies sat with tight blue gowns stretched across them. There were no other children. Paramedics wheeled an old woman in through the back door. She was strapped to a gurney and yelling at the men who may have even saved her life. She found Domingo and they locked eyes. Help me!

In the morning the doctors admitted Theo. They moved him to the second floor, room E225, a private room with a view of the parking lot. Theo wanted his mother to hold his hand. Domingo stood next to her mother and watched as a nurse held a stethoscope to Theo's chest. The nurse was a short, middle-aged woman. Her nametag said Clarissa. She moved slowly and deliberately.

"How is he?" asked the mother.

Clarissa didn't respond to the mother's question. She began connecting a small, thin tube to the plastic tube which protruded from beneath the skin on Theo's arm. She hooked the tube up to a machine and started pressing buttons.

"What are you doing?" asked the mother.

There was no interruption to Clarissa's movements as she adjusted the bag on the metal pole by Theo's bed.

The mother stepped around the bed, putting herself deliberately next to Clarissa. "Where's the doctor?" she asked.

It was enough to prompt Clarissa to clear her throat. Another nurse rushed into the room, speaking excitedly about a different patient. They left the mother standing there with no immediate answers to her questions.

Domingo opened a folding chair she had found in the hallway and set it next to Theo's bed. She made her mother sit. She asked if she needed anything. The room was silent, except for the sound of one of the monitors near Theo's bed. It beeped whenever the numbers on the screen dipped below seventy-five.

Almost one fifteen. Domingo was hungry. Her mother gave her money. She entered the elevator, punching a button to take her to the basement. She followed the signs to the cafeteria. There were vending machines next to the wall and a place to return dirty dishes. A long line had formed at the grill station where they cooked to order. She lingered by a group of teenagers in yellow shirts and white pants.

She took a sandwich to a table in the corner. She draped her jacket over the back of the chair. She ate and listened to a conversation from the table next to hers.

"But they said it was an abscess."

"Well, it wasn't. They got the pathology report yesterday. It had cancer cells."

"How did that happen?"

"No one knows. They cut it out best they could and now it's grown back twice the size."

"How can he swallow?"

"He manages. I just hope he doesn't bite it while he's chewing."

"That's sickening."

"I know. He wants to show you what it looks like, but I told him to keep his mouth shut."

"I don't want to look at it."

"Well, if you do it's this dark gray thing between his cheek and gum."

Domingo missed school so that she could be with Theo and her mother. Two more days went by and they took turns sitting by Theo's bedside. When it wasn't her turn, Domingo sat in the waiting room, reading all the magazines. When she wasn't sitting she explored the rest of the hospital. She took the elevator to each floor. She found the cardiac floor, the cancer floor, and the place where they took people's x-rays. She found the hospital pharmacy and watched the pharmacist move among aisles of boxes, bottles, and tubes.

Every day she ate at the cafeteria. She liked to sit near the doctors and nurses. She watched with interest the volunteers in yellow shirts and white pants.

One day Domingo saw one of the volunteers sitting at a table in the atrium. She knew who he was because he was wearing a yellow shirt and white pants. She picked up a magazine, but instead of reading it she kept looking at him. He had dark green eyes, curly brown hair, and nice white teeth.

"Excuse me," she said to him. "Are you a volunteer?"

"Yes," he said. "A bunch of us from church help around the hospital."

"Doing what?"

"Clerical stuff, mostly. On occasion we get to work directly with patients. We help move them about, get them to and from their cars, make sure they don't get lost. Essentially, we try to make their stay here comfortable."

"So you work for free."

He grinned. "We get lunch."

Domingo nodded.

"Are you visiting here?" he asked.

"Yeah, my brother Theo."

"Hope he's okay."

"Me too," she said, but her voice dropped. And that was the thing. She didn't really know how he was doing. She kept asking her mother and she wouldn't say anything. Domingo was worried that they were keeping crucial information from her. She thought they know something, but they didn't want to tell her. Her mother spent most of the time by his bed and even stayed overnight twice in a row. They couldn't stay here forever. Her mother had to return to work and Domingo couldn't miss many more days of school.

"Do you go to school around here?" she asked the volunteer.

"Across the lake," he said. "Eastside Prep. A private high school."

Domingo had never heard of the school. She attended a public high school in North Seattle. In two years she would graduate. She dreamed of art school, assuming she could afford to pay the tuition. It was not cheap. That dream seemed a long way off. She had missed several days already and she would need to make up a lot of homework. It would be so hard.

The young man looked at his watch and stood up. He excused himself and she said goodbye. She watched him walk away. He was nice, pleasant. She took the elevator back up to the second floor. Theo was still sleeping. Her mother had left the room. Domingo sat by Theo's side holding his hand. He was having difficulty breathing.

Flu, then pneumonia, a viral infection that could have spread to the brain. Still no word on a cure for Theo. He slept most days and screamed at night, which worried the nurses. For three days their mother slept in a chair by Theo's bed. Domingo had not seen her so distraught, so worried. She invented reasons for her mother to get up and leave the room. Finally, she convinced her mother to sleep in the visitor's room down the hall.

One afternoon her mother's boss called on the phone in Theo's room. Her mother stood next to Theo, running her fingertips through his hair while she pleaded with her boss to let her stay for a few more days.

After her mother hung up the phone, Domingo asked, "Can't you get another job? One with a nice boss?"

"He's really a thoughtful man," said her mother.

"Not if he doesn't understand Theo's sick."

Her mother shook her head. "When I go back to work," she said, "You'll have to sit with Theo."

"What about school?" Domingo asked. "How am I going to finish if I'm not in school?"

"I'll talk to your teachers," said the mother.

"But how will I do the work later?"

Her mother had no answers.

Domingo curled up in a chair in the corner of Theo's room, slipping her feet underneath her bottom. It had been over a week since her mother went back to work. In a minute she was asleep and dreaming. She was walking Theo to school.

"You look good today, sis," he said to her. "You need to pick me up by the flagpole."

"I know. Three o'clock."

Theo poked his half-sister in the ribs. "How could you know that?"

How could she not? Her mother made sure she knew what to do, reminding her of things she had already mentioned before. Her mother made sure she understood what to do and when to do it. That was how things worked. That was her life.

A nurse woke her up. "Theo has slipped into a coma."

Domingo started shaking, like when she had the flu last summer. The nurse held her hand and she walked her to Theo's room. Two doctors were leaning over Theo's bed. One was looking in his eyes with a flashlight. The other was sticking a needle into the plastic tube running into his arm. She overheard the doctor say that his brain was shutting down. Domingo collapsed onto the floor. They had to revive her by putting something in her nose. It smelled bad. She fought back, pushing her arms out, pushing the nurses away.

She screamed. "Help him, please."

A nurse grabbed her by the arm, trying to calm her.

"What are you doing? Help him now. Help him. Please God. You've got to help him."

"Where's his mother?" said one of the doctors.

"At work," said a nurse. She called for another nurse.

Domingo pushed her way through the doctors until she stood at the side of Theo's bed. She held onto the railing. A nurse tried to pull her back, away from the bed. Domingo lunged at her, almost knocking her over. Only the doctor could hold her back.

"Help my brother," she said.

Why were they focused on her? Why could they not see that he was in trouble? He could die. She pleaded with them to help Theo. She said that she would forgive them for all the things she thought they had done wrong if only they would fix him and make him better. Make him better. Make the pain go away. Cure him. She fought for that and she kept on fighting until they brought in someone to take care of her, someone who wasn't a nurse. Someone wearing a yellow shirt and white pants.

She recognized him. The young man from the atrium cafeteria. The young man in a yellow shirt with dark green eyes, curly brown hair and nice white teeth. He helped her to her feet and led her from the room. He took her down a long corridor. The lights were bright and he shielded her eyes by holding his arm above her head. He opened a door and they entered a quiet room. It was a chapel. She recognized the picture on the wall as the picture of Jesus. She wept when she saw it.

The young man told her his name. Saunto. He led her to a pew. He sat down beside her and put his arm around her shoulders and she kept looking past him to the picture of Jesus on the wall. Jesus was weeping too, and Domingo shuddered, knowing that in some way she was to blame for Theo being sick and Jesus crying. Saunto said he would pray with her. In between sobs, she thanked him for wanting to pray, but she said she would pray for Theo by herself. She prayed to God and to the picture of Jesus on the wall to save Theo from pain and suffering. She prayed that Theo would get better. The young man waited beside her. She prayed that his affliction would be cleansed and he would be free of all misery. For Theo's sake she prayed. Amen.

Domingo was sitting in the chapel with Saunto. He held her in his arms. She kept looking past him to the picture of Jesus on the wall. Jesus was looking at her. Jesus was watching. She heard Jesus telling her that she was to blame for Theo's illness. You must be punished for your sins, he said. You must repent, he said. You must confess your sins. She would confess, she thought. She would confess her sins and Jesus would see that she was not an evil person and then he would save Theo.

"I was sitting cross-legged on the floor while Theo sat in the bathtub," she said to Saunto. "There was mildew on the walls and around the edges of the porcelain. Theo sprayed foam cleaner on the green and black tiles. He was on his hands and knees scrubbing the tiles with an old washcloth. After he rinsed the black bubbles down the drain, I washed the black bubbles from his hair with shampoo. And that's when he started coughing. I don't remember if I opened the window, but I have an awful feeling I didn't. I heard him coughing and throwing up again, and then Mother called."

Domingo told him everything. Saunto was patient listening to her confession. She felt his tolerance. She told him that she panicked when Theo threw up. Her mother had told her a hundred times, he's special. He has allergies. Be careful of this, be careful of that. Then here he was, coughing up mucus. She told Saunto about lying to her mother when she called from work. She didn't want to lie. She knew how important her mother's job was, how they needed money to eat and pay rent. She knew lying was wrong. It was a sin to lie. But it was a necessary sin because she didn't think Theo was really sick, not sick enough for their mother to leave work and come home. Ever since her father had left them, Domingo worried about her family. She worried about them staying together. She had been worried for so long that when Theo started coughing and throwing up, she knew she had to take care of him. Her mother was doing her part by working. That's why when her mother called she told her everything was all right. She had told her mother this while she had her arm wrapped around Theo's shoulders. She had told her mother they were playing games in the living room. Monopoly. "He owns Boardwalk and Park Place," she'd said. She smiled down at Theo while she lied. His face had developed small pink blisters. She put him in bed. She put little white socks on his feet and covered him with a blue blanket, his favorite. She gave him a pat on his head and squeezed his hand. She held his hand tight when he began to cough. She felt relieved when the spasms subsided and he fell asleep like nothing was wrong. She turned out the overhead light and shut the door quietly.

Somewhere in the middle of all the coughs and throwing up her mother called again. The lie took on further permanence. Her mother wanted to speak with Theo. There was no lie this time when she told her that he was asleep. "Go back to work," Domingo said. She hung up the phone, but she stood there waiting for it to ring again. Mothers have powers other people don't have, she thought. They hear conversations. But the phone was silent. Her mother was busy.

She had everything under control. She checked on Theo throughout most of the night. Only once did she get scared when she touched his skin. It was hot and his clothes were sticking to his arms and legs. Fever. She knew that her mother was just a phone call away and that she should use the phone. She pulled down the blanket and removed his socks. Theo started crying for his momma. That started her crying. She sat next to him on his bed waiting for her mother to come home from work. She heard every sound in the apartment. She waited for the sound of the key in the lock.

Saunto brought her a glass of water. He brushed a

hair away from her face. "Are you okay now?" he asked. Was there anything else she wanted to say?

"Yes," she said. "I want to tell my mother that I'm sorry."

CUL-DE-SAC

The new house has a high-pitched roof like the peak of an old barn. The room I'm standing in is small and cramped. Its windows are tall and narrow. The carpet is stained and a musty odor lingers. My sister pokes her head in the doorway, her eyes narrowing suspiciously at something in the room. I follow her down the hallway to her room, but she closes the door in my face. I start down the stairs and hear Chuck's voice. It fills the void of the empty house. I surprise them in the kitchen. They're standing real close. Mom leans into his shoulder, her palm flat against the sleeve of his jacket, kissing him on the cheek. He turns to kiss her back and her mouth opens slightly. She sees me looking and steps back.

We're days from moving in and Chuck is giving us a tour. Chuck is our realtor and he's standing by the kitchen island, his large hands spread out on black granite marble.

"I love the hardwood floors," says Mom.

"And there's recessed lighting and vaulted ceilings," Chuck says. "It's got plenty of room, a big backyard, and a gas range."

Mom looks at me. I turn and go out the front door. I'm not at all happy we're moving. There was nothing wrong with the old place.

Out on the sidewalk in front of the house, I look up and down the street. We're in a cul-de-sac with about four or five homes bordering the semi-circle. All are painted white.

Mom and Chuck come out the front door. Lisa walks around to the front from the corner of the house. She must have come out the side gate. I follow her to Chuck's car, a ten-year-old, burgundy-colored Mercedes. Both of us climb into the back seat. Neither of us says much other than to look out at Mom and Chuck who are still standing on the front porch. The wind blows my mother's long brown hair about her face. Chuck closes the front door and locks it. He places the key in the lock box.

That evening Mom comes home from the title company. She shows us a sheaf of papers and her signatures.

"We own the house," she says. "Let's celebrate."

She cooks a big meal, but I'm not hungry. I move the food around on my plate like a little boy. Part of me wants to scream and the other part wants my mom to be happy. I can't seem to have it both ways.

After dinner I slip out the back door and sit on the cement steps leading down into the yard. I hear the scraping of nails, the sounds of earth being moved, pebbles and stones in motion. The dog is digging again, underneath the fence. I whistle and he comes over, jumping on me as his tail whips back and forth. His front paws are dirty and cold. He's expecting me to throw a stick or something.

It's getting late when the door opens behind me.

"Come inside," says Mom.

My friend Darrel and his girlfriend, Angela, come over with sorry tears in their eyes. Darrel doesn't want me to move, and he blames my father, as if he's running us out of the neighborhood. We're in my bedroom. Darrel lies on his back, on the mattress with Angela tucked alongside him.

"We could rig the brakes on his truck," he says. "Or loosen the lug nuts on his wheels."

"Oh, Darrel," says Angela. "Quit joking."

"Really, it would be so easy. Where did he move to, Randy? We find out where he parks at night, we can mess him up real bad. We dress like ninjas. All black. Masks. Those hooded sweatshirts you see on that Cops movie. We'll just loosen three of the lugs on each wheel. Maybe drain some of the brake fluid for good measure."

He talks of launching a frontal assault on my father, a talk that includes potential illegal activities involving guns, knives, and ropes.

"I got fireworks from last July," says Darrel. "From my brother Paul."

"There was a ban on fireworks last year," says Angela.

"Apparently not," says Darrel. He's smiling like he

pulled off some caper.

Angela sits up. "Lisa must feel bad. She'll miss Jerome."

"They're just friends."

Angela looks at Darrel, then back to me. "More than that. Everybody knows they're doing it."

"My little sister?"

"It's just gossip," says Darrel. "Jerome likes to brag."

I say, "She ain't doing it with Jerome or anybody. You should tell him to shut his face."

Lisa is upstairs listening to music in her room. Her door is open and I stand in the doorway. She's writing in her journal.

"Can I read that some time?" I ask.

"Get out of my room, creep," she says.

It's Saturday night and Mom drops me off at the bowling alley on her way to work. She has the night shift this weekend and she doesn't like when I sit at home alone. I find Darrel in a game of pool with an older guy by the name of Arlee. Arlee's usually around trying to get a game going for money. Darrel tells me to keep quiet, peering down the shaft of his cue stick. I survey the table and see that he's trying to bank the seven into the side pocket, but he misses and Arlee smirks. Darrel says, "Crap." But I know it's all for show. Darrel's strategy is to make the other guy think he's a lousy shooter.

"Rack 'em up," says Darrel.

Arlee pulls a twenty out of his wallet and lays it on the pool table.

Darrel digs two tens from his shirt pocket and covers Arlee's twenty. It's his turn to break and he smashes the cue ball into the number one and the ten with the blue stripe falls into the corner pocket. Darrel works the table efficiently. He's serious now. He has this intense look about him. His eyes squint and he's working his tongue around inside his mouth. He's tough when he isn't being so friendly.

Later, we're sitting at a booth in The Grill and Darrel pulls three twenties from his pocket. "That Arlee sucks at pool," he says. "I had him right from the break. I bet he goes home tonight thinking he could beat me next time."

Angela works the counter serving burgers and fries to the moonlight bowlers. She comes over and slides a plate of curly fries across the table.

"Hey, can you fetch me a Coke?" asks Darrel.

"We going for beer later?" asks Angela.

"Paul's meeting us across the street at Tuckers. He'll get the beer."

Angela blows him a kiss. "Your brother is so cool."

When her shift is over she slides in next to me. Her bare arm brushes mine. I like when she sits close. I glance at Darrel, but he doesn't notice. Angela has been his girl forever. She smiles at me and I'm not so glad we all decide to go outside to the parking lot.

We wait for Paul outside in the back parking lot at Tuckers Grocery. We're joined by Nelson and Luis, brothers who live near Darrel in the River Bend Apartments. Luis is riding his bike in a zigzag pattern and everyone is talking to me about the move.

"You can live with us," Nelson says. "But you'd have to sleep with my sister." He laughs.

"She's not your type," says Darrel.

Nelson throws a fake punch at Darrel's mid-section. "Yours either."

Darrel reaches over and strikes Nelson on the arm and then slaps him on top of the head. He shoves Nelson who bumps into me. He tells me to get out of the way.

I try to hit him on the side of the head. "Don't ever talk like that," I say. "Don't ever talk to me like that, you shit."

That's when we see Paul's car.

Paul drives a '68 Chevy Impala, lowered, with deep dish rims and a creamy-yellow paint job. He gets out of the car and the first thing he does is hug Angela, giving Darrel a big grin. Angela laughs, but I think she likes the attention, probably even likes Paul's long blond hair, which is shoulder length. Even though Paul has graduated, he likes to hang out with us. We're a tight group.

"Where's the beer?" he asks.

I point to the back door at Tuckers. "I haven't seen Jerome yet. He's supposed to bring out the beer when he makes his trash run."

Paul is upset about the beer and then the back door opens at Tuckers. Jerome walks out, carrying a big box, headed for the dumpster. He's wearing a blue apron that falls to the knees. His jeans are long and the ends are frayed and soiled. I walk over to him.

"Where is it?"

"Paul never paid me," says Jerome.

I look to Paul who is walking slowly towards us.

"He isn't going to give us beer," I say.

Jerome ignores us and takes his box over to the dumpster. When he bends down to pull dead lettuce heads from the box, Darrel rears up on the bike like a jockey on a mad thoroughbred and propels himself and the bike right into Jerome's back, knocking him to the ground and sending heads of lettuce in every direction. I pull Jerome to his feet by his apron, but Jerome punches me in the stomach and then Darrel is there pulling on his hair, dragging him to the ground. Darrel gets him on his back and straddles his chest. He has his arms and legs pinned. Angela is screaming and Jerome is crying. Paul yanks on Darrel's jacket and pulls him away. Jerome's lip is bleeding. There are pieces of green lettuce leaves on the front of his apron. I'm still sore and take a swing at Jerome's chin and just glance it with my knuckles. It isn't enough to knock him down and he sprints off towards the back door at Tuckers. Nobody chases him.

Strangely, I watch my mother prepare to move as if I'm seeing it all from a distance. Her plan to organize and throw away the things we don't need, to pack our belongings in a neat, orderly manner, making sure to label everything and assign a location, to stack and relocate all movable items to the garage, makes me dizzy. Maybe it's because I'm not helping that sets the focal point of my vision back to where it is now, a point where I am detached from the actual preparation. I watch her wrap plates and glassware in brown paper and stack boxes in the corner of the living room. I witness a half-hearted approach to cleaning out closets that resembles a poorly executed garage sale in which only a portion of the junk that was intended to sell ever makes it out of the garage, only to be put back into storage on a shelf or in a pile with the other remnants of a colorful life.

Chuck stops by the house one day when Mom is away. He knocks on the front door, but walks inside anyway. I'm sitting on the sofa watching a movie and he tells me to come for a ride with him and my sister. I tell him I'm not going anywhere. He rushes over to where I'm sitting and grabs my arm.

"Get in the car, Randy," he says.

I look past him and see Lisa standing by the front door with her arms crossed, shoulders all bunched up like she's cold. Something is definitely wrong and it makes me nervous.

"What's going on?"

"Randy," says Chuck. "We're taking your sister downtown."

He looks serious. I follow them outside and get in the car. Lisa's sitting in the back seat. She won't look at me.

Chuck starts the car. He's backing out of the driveway when he says, "She's pregnant."

"What?"

He turns his head briefly, still trying to keep his eyes on the road. "She's just a kid, Randy. Kids can't raise babies."

I sit back and try to think. I'm shocked.

Chuck is silent, just drives.

"Have you told Mom? Please, just talk with her."

I can sense her trying to make some excuse, but she cannot find the words. She recoils when I try to grab her hand.

"Let go of me," she says. "Let go of me."

We pass the hospital and Chuck turns the corner and goes up the hill. He pulls the Mercedes into the parking lot next to a brick building into a space in front of a door where the sign reads Pacific Medical Arts. The art of what? I think.

"Stay in the car," says Chuck.

"Lisa, wait. Don't do it."

Lisa shakes her head. She's determined to get out and that's when Chuck walks to her door and opens it. Then they're gone inside, leaving me alone in the car. I stare at the building. She's invisible to me now. I want her to come back out, to change her mind, to think of the possibilities.

An hour passes. It's been a terrible day. The whole week has been a waste. We've all been busy packing up our stuff. Mom is so preoccupied that she doesn't know how fragile her family has become. I'm still not happy about moving or the prospect of spending even more time with Chuck. He lives closer to the new house and will be visiting us more than usual. I just don't want to end up living with him. I blame Chuck partly because he came into our lives at a time where my Mom needed someone. Not since my father left has she been so vulnerable. My parent's divorce is recent, but their hate for one another had long been established by the time he lost his job. After that we never knew when he would come home, day or night, and every time he did, we were anxious. Where had he been? What hadn't worked out this time? What would he do now?

Like the time I looked past my father into the driveway where he'd driven the car up onto the lawn after visiting a bar.

His car knocked over a planter full of dead geraniums; then I saw my sister's bicycle underneath the car, crushed and mangled. He brushed past me, pushing me with his arm either to force me out of the way or to steady himself. I stayed in the garage and I heard them yelling and screaming inside. For a second I thought I heard my sister's voice, but I'd remembered she was over at a friend's house and I was glad she wasn't there. A glass shattered on the floor and it went on like this for a while; it never stopped, and then my mother came out and ran across the street to the neighbors. I opened the door to the laundry room and heard my father in the kitchen. He was panting like a sick dog, breathing heavy, and I thought he was having a heart attack. He grabbed onto the counter with both hands and leaned over at the waist looking straight down at the floor. I realized he was throwing up. When he was done he looked up and saw me, and wiped his mouth with the sleeve on his red and black, plaid shirt. He opened the refrigerator and grabbed a beer and I followed him through the living room to the front door. It was chained and when he yanked on the door he pulled the screws right out of the doorframe. He lurched out onto the front lawn where everyone from the neighborhood had gathered.

Someone called the cops and while my father tried

to start his car they pulled up behind him. One of them hit the siren, on and off, and then they were out and standing alongside the car ordering him to get out slowly. But he'd locked the doors and it was no use trying to coax him. The one cop, who was the junior varsity football coach a few years ago, took out his baton and rammed the end of it through the driver's side window, sending bits of glass everywhere, but mostly into the car. My father yelled and cussed and lost the battle for his keys.

No words are spoken between us as I walk Lisa up to her room. She lies down on her bed. As I pull a blanket over her, I see there are no pictures on the walls, no books on her desk. The room is as sterile as the one she just left behind. I look at her and wonder what is going through her mind. I can't imagine the pain inside her head or in her heart. It is a pain made worse by the fact we're moving in less than a week.

A few nights later all of my friends decide to take a ride. We wait until Angela gets off work. Outside the bowling alley we all pile into Paul's car: Darrel, Angela, Nelson, Paul and me. We're hardly in the seat when Paul pulls out onto the street, gunning the engine and loosening the gravel underneath the back wheels. We're heading north up the freeway towards Seattle. I'm in the back seat, behind Paul. Angela and Darrel are practically humping next to me and every now and then Angela's elbow pokes me in the side and I can tell she's doing it on purpose.

"Where we going, brother?" yells Darrel.

"Nowhere," says Paul and sometime later Nelson,

who's sitting up front with Paul, says he's hungry. Paul takes the James Street exit and we head down the hill toward the waterfront. Darrel wants to eat somewhere in Pioneer Square, but Paul keeps on driving. We're stopped at an intersection underneath the Alaska Way viaduct, and while we're waiting for a street trolley to pass Nelson shouts obscenities to a guy walking with two girls. The guy points a finger at Nelson. He keeps on giving us a shitty look and only moves out of the way when Paul inches the fender into his leg. We're a block past the fish fry place that Nelson wants to try when Angela spots a parking stall. Paul turns the Chevy around and by the time we get to it, the spot is taken. We decide not to eat downtown and Paul takes us back up the hill to I-5 and heads north again. He turns east and starts out across one of the floating bridges.

We're heading to Bellevue when Darrel says we should go see our new house.

"What for?" I ask.

"No reason."

So we drive through Bellevue to Redmond and head to an area of homes and neighborhoods on a plateau overlooking a lake. In the dark it is hard to find the right street, but I do and tell Paul to drive slowly.

Nelson sees it first.

Angela says she likes it.

Paul has no opinion.

Darrel says nothing, and in fact it is his silence that provokes me to ask him what's wrong with the house. He looks at me and his eyes are wide open. A small laugh escapes. He's serious about something.

"Go to the end of the street and turn around," he tells his brother.

Paul pulls out of the cul-de-sac and drives to the end of the street. He turns the Chevy around, pulling over to the curb before shutting the engine off.

"What are we doing?"

Paul turns around, leaning over the edge of the seat.

"Tell me about Chuck," he says. "Is he still hanging around?"

"Yeah," I say. "He's like an alligator. He's clamped down on my Mom's leg and won't let go."

Nelson giggles from the front seat. "He's an interloper, Randy."

Darrel grabs Nelson's jacket sleeve. "Don't use those fancy words in my brother's car, okay?"

He turns to Angela. "Interloper. Yeah, that's good."

He looks at me. "I'm still pissed you're leaving," he says. "It's time to make things right. I got contingency plans."

"What plans?"

"You said you didn't want to move."

"Yeah, but what are we doing?"

"I'm helping you," he says.

He climbs out of the car, telling Paul to pop the trunk. He goes around behind the car and I try looking out the back window, but it's too dark to see anything. Darrel grabs something from the trunk and takes off running to the new house. I get out and follow him, running after a shadow that disappears through the gate on the side of the garage. I find him breaking the window on the side door. He reaches through the hole in the window and unlatches the door lock. I follow him. Inside the air smells chalky and clings to the back of my throat. I'm surprised to see a car parked inside. It's Chuck's Mercedes. Darrel runs his hand over the smooth, polished surface, the cheap ring on his finger leaving a scratch from tail fender to front bumper. He holds up a can of gasoline and jeers. He twists off the cap and tosses it into the corner. Recognition comes slowly, too slow, but I can see it now and there is a sudden weight in my heart as heavy as my feet. Darrel douses the hood of the car with gas. The smell is pungent and strong. He pulls a lighter out of his pocket and holds it out.

"Take it," he says.

It's one of those small, butane lighters. My father would have a lighter like this. He'd have several. One in his shirt pocket. One in his truck. One in his bedroom for when he smoked in bed. He's probably in bed right now. Drunk or asleep. He would be wearing one of his plaid shirts. I can see him lying there in the dark. I flick the button and a tiny orange flame lights up the garage. I can see an image of my father's face in the fire dancing at the end of my finger. Something is happening that we can't take back. As the angry flames spread, the burgundy-colored paint congeals into the crumpled, blackened shapes of dead sunflowers with rivulets of smoke rising up to the ceiling.

ABOUT THE AUTHOR

MATTHEW GALLANT is a graduate of Seattle Pacific University where he earned the degree of Master of Fine Arts in Creative Writing - Fiction.